COYOTE DREAMS

Susan Nunes   illustrated by Ronald Himler

ATHENEUM   NEW YORK

Atheneum
Macmillan Publishing Company
866 Third Avenue, New York, NY 10022
Collier Macmillan Canada, Inc.
Printed in Japan

10   9   8   7   6   5   4   3   2

Library of Congress Cataloging-in-Publication Data

Nunes, Susan, date.
Coyote dreams/Susan Nunes; illustrated by Ronald Himler.—1st ed.
p.   cm.
Summary: At night coyotes come quietly to a suburban garden,
bringing with them their special, magical desert world.
ISBN 0-689-31398-5
[1. Coyotes—Fiction.   2. Deserts—Fiction.]   I. Himler, Ronald,
ill.   II. Title.
PZ7.N9645Co   1988
[E]—dc19
87-30288   CIP   AC

To Adam, Mirah, and Jamil

They come by night when the house is still
and the garden is blue and gray.

They come by night when the moon is full
and city lights are far away.

Out of the shadows of elkhorn fern, by the path
near the garden wall, a twig snaps, a pebble rolls.

"Who's there?" you call.

One, two, three, and four. One, two, three, and four.
One, two, three, and...more.

Coyotes!

Whisper their name the ancient way,
"Coyotl. Coyotl."

Where, where is the garden wall?
Sand and sagebrush are desert things!

Where, where are swings and slide, and
gypsy moths drawn to the light?

Lizards, bats, and mountain cats…

rocks, caves, and silver hills…

moonlight on a buzzard's wings.

These are what coyotes bring.

Whisper their name the ancient way,
"Coyotl. Coyotl."

You are in their desert world!
Coyotes dance.

Coyotes play.

Coyotes sing such lonely songs.

Yellow eyes and pointed faces,
they sit in a ring and tell their tales,

tales that take you far away

to other times

and other places.

Whisper their name the ancient way,
"Coyotl. Coyotl."

When you're sleepy, they say good night.
One, two, three, and four. One, two, three, and four.
One, two, three, and...more coyotes!

Here again is the garden wall.

Here again are swings and slide,

and gypsy moths drawn to the light.
Where, where are sand and sagebrush?
Where are all the desert things?
Lizards, bats, and mountain cats?

Rocks, caves, and silver hills, moonlight on a buzzard's wings?
Gone again to desert places!

One, two, three, and four. One, two, three, and four.
One, two, three…no more.

But…whisper their name the ancient way, "Coyotl. Coyotl."

And sometimes they will leave a story,
old as a coyote dream. Let it fill your desert places.

"Coyotl. Coyotl."